Deeply Rooted:
Seeds

JAMAL LEON JACKSON

A message from me to you,

I am average. I am boring. I am growing, and growth can sometimes be boring. If only this were boring, it would all be made up and not real.

I am the main character in these pieces, as I have always been. I used to be very expressive, and then seven years ago, I turned the feeling off, the emotion, off. Here in this book, you'll find me trying to express messages to you. Each piece has a huge set of meanings and messages that are hidden in each line. They are designed so that the more you (the reader) knows about me (the writer) the more you can uncover within the pieces. I call them "pieces" because they are pieces of me, that I never intended on showing to the world or at least, I didn't believe there was anything worth showing. While reading take your time, allow your initial thoughts to spark your secondary thoughts and then challenge those thoughts. Each piece will attempt to confuse or lose you completely. I am eager to see who stays with each one, who gets lost, and what is found in the place you were lost in. The pieces themselves have a voice that flows through each lines trying to break out, and be heard. In each piece, that voice is being muffled by the rubble that is my life. Under that rubble is everything I have, and am or maybe the rubble is all that is left. These pieces are a roadmap to the location of that rubble, and hopefully, will help those looking to dig me out.

Roots for trees are the strong bonds that hold them together, feeding nutrients throughout the branches and leaves. For me, these roots have me held captive, and being deeply rooted is the opposite of freedom. "Deeply Rooted" is a book series that will have at least three volumes. Seeds, Roots, and Blooming. (For now, but the goal is nine.) "Seeds" is the beginning, what caused everything, and a window into the outside garden I am creating or that is creating me.

Here, I am the love addict, the servant, the criminal, the victim, the hero that couldn't save himself, the devil that wanted to push himself, the lonely, the hurt, the hurtful, and the hidden.

CONTENTS

Acknowledgments   I

1   Numb   7-11

2   My Pulse   12-18

3   Ashes   19-28

4   Heartless   29-33

5   Heart Felt   34-40

6   A Hard Spot   41-44

7   Kerosene Killer   45-48

8   Try Again, King   49-53

9   Enigma   54-60

10   Gasping   61-64

About the author   65

ACKNOWLEDGMENTS

Thank you.

To my photographer Joseph Fuentes, who without hesitation helped me capture every image you see in this book, to capture me.

To my graphic designer Cameron Moore, who used his pen and pencil to create these characters in a way my mind needed.

To my readers along the years that cried at lines that made me cringe. That pushed me to publish this book, even when I felt like it wasn't worthy.

To my mother Koneda Jackson, who kept me from falling when I tripped, pushed me when I held back, and constantly reminded me that "You are a button away from being an author. What is taking you so long? Push it."

&

To every real person in this book that created these traumas. Thank you for being the darkness that pulled me down, or the light that burned me. You all might deserve the most praise, if not for you building the ugly, the beautiful would not have been birthed.

So THANK YOU. This isn't, wasn't, and won't be anything without you.

NUMB

I'm waiting

I've been waiting

I'm waiting

I've been waiting

She said patience is a virtue...

And they said patience cannot hurt... you...

I've been waiting to tell my story...

And my waiting is hurting,

Is it not strong enough...

Have I... in my past not been wrong enough..

I was ok but on the edge of my seat.. when she sang.. when her feet hit that pine wood mixed with poplar tree...

Fighting... she kept fighting...

Fighting... I've been fighting.. what have I been fighting?

My breath was at the tip of my lips...

My heart raced...

A feeling of oversight... a feeling I've taught myself... to keep out of sight... a feeling... my feeling...

My feelings.. hidden behind my dark dealings..

My feelings...

My dealings...

My feelings...

My dealings...

My dealer... who dealt me my feelings... you dealt me my feelings...

I'm afraid to cry now... but why now...

Deeply Rooted: Seeds

I'm afraid to cry now...

I'm afraid to cry now...

I'm afraid to break down...

You broke me down...

My dealer.. you dealt me...

My feelings you dealt with for me...

The feelings you dealt with for me...

My dealer...

My dealer...

My healer...

My ... no her... no my... no her... no my..

No our... make up... our concealer...

My feelings... my dealings...

My feelings...

My dealer ... dealing in my feelings...

Called me crazy...

My dealer called my feelings crazy...

Then held out his hand... with drugs to suppress me...

And in his voice... his eyes.. head held up high...

He said "get high, and just pay me."

You're crazy...

My feelings...

My dealings...

Blazing hot outside... blazing hot outside...

Blazing hot outside...

But this fact.. still so chilling...

The dealer...

My dealer confused... with a healer... he cured me of my weakness...

Of my feelings...

He cured me of my illness...

My dealer.. my feelings... the feeling of my dealer...

He dealt me what I asked for... I mean I asked for it...

I asked for this... I asked for this...

I asked for this!

My dealer... I asked for this...

My dealer... said I asked for this...

My feelings, but my dealings...

I asked my dealer...

Where did you put my feelings?

Panicking, snatching, patience attacking,

I want them back!!

Screaming,

I want my feelings back!!

It's blazing hot... and I want the feeling back...

I want to feel the heat against my back, like hot coal,

Lava, like being scolded, or being controlled,

I don't feel healed...

I don't,

I don't feel...

Where are my feelings?

You are my dealer, right? Well where are they?

Deal me my fucking feelings...

Deeply Rooted: Seeds

Deal me...

Deal me...

Deal me...

Deal me... my feelings...

Can you please... please just deal me my feelings?

I want to feel them, pain, fear, these stab wounds,

I want my feelings...

Even the drugs you gave me... I can't feel them...

Even the drugs,

you gave me...

I can't feel them...

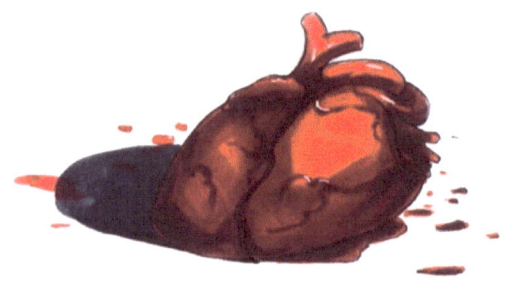

MY PULSE

I can't keep this up,

There's blood all over me but none of you can see it,

It's dripping,

Drip Drop,

I'm bleeding out,

My heart is bleeding out,

My mind is bleeding out,

There's blood pouring from my mouth,

My wrists are bleeding,

My sanity is fleeing,

There's blood everywhere you just can't see it,

If I bleed out, or live...

What's the difference?

I feel like a ghost, alive but unseen,

Floating around, some can see me but most can't feel me,

Some can feel me but choose to not see me,

What's the point of being a ghost?

And for the ones that can't see and feel, I catch myself doing the most,

When you choose not to break bread, I make sure we have toast,

A toast, lets toast, a toast is in order,

Why?

To celebrate,

But celebrate what? Celebrate our friendship?

A full course meal, to celebrate,

Celebrate what? My censorship?

Celebrate what?

"Do you know who I am?"

I asked this,

Your reply, "well you have to show me"

Does a pot of gold come to you?

Does the job you've always wanted, search for you? Apply for you?

No, but in this case you want more work?

More work from me?

Why does this not apply to you?

What do you know about me?

Steady contact, describing my flaws and faults..

Is this steady contact, explanations of a contract, or my mind and heart losing contact?

Have you any idea who we are?

My eyes began to show me the truth, that as I spilled these questions, so did more blood spill from me,

I'm bleeding again,

There's a puddle of blood in my trunk,

There's blood on the seats,

Blood gushing from my teeth,

There's blood at the base of my feet,

There's blood on my thumbs when I text you,

There's blood all over my body, but you use your eyes to see through,

There's blood in my day to day,

There's blood when you misunderstand the things I say,

Drowning in blood,

I went to the hospital, they sent me back...

Deeply Rooted: Seeds

Apparently drowning in blood and depression wasn't taken as a serious attack,

I try to give signals, use life but no answer,

Can you pinpoint when my blood boils?

Can you understand the point of a winning battle with no spoils?

What can you do if not drain?

Expectations and representations...

You expect my dead body to dance and do tricks, while you wash your hands and the blades you used,

It's, "crazy"

How can your expectations overpower my own? Overpower me? How can you care more about how we talk and not if it is hard for me to talk? To speak.

But these are things I must teach?

I simply desired friends and counterparts, that were within my reach...

This is actually for me, and not for you...

I had not drowned yet, even with blood everywhere, I had not been found yet,

So I needed to write down what this blood could do,

And a shower,

To wash the blood away, but deep down I think washing away the blood, washes away my power, washes away me,

There's blood in every word I use to explain my frustrations to you,

I didn't know blood could taste this sour, this ripe, this wrong, this right,

Even after the 10th and you still don't understand,

But my consideration and my "getting used to you" is something you command,

Something you demand,

And I question if I can,

If I can get past you not seeing the blood in my eyes,

If I can get past the blood in my hands after each try,

If I can forget the blood in my teeth, the blood that fed me...

When you wouldn't,

The blood of memories over money,

Sometimes I wished I spent more money to erase these memories,

Unprepared that they would burn more than nightmares,

The friends I have to beg to contact me...

The friends I shared ink with, and then were gone before I could blink,

The friends I can hear the liquid pour from the bottle for,

The friends I watered and like a plant cared for,

The friends that were scared of more.

The friends that were afraid of my blood on the floor,

Of me,

The blood I let drip from these veins, to stop you from feeling pain..

I'm the friend you gave all your secrets too...

The friend you stated knew the most and best of you,

But what does it matter?

Why run a race with no trophy? To only be met by your laughter?

Who does that?

Who comes and goes?

What hurt comes and goes?

Leaves an imprint on another, provides stories and shares worries..

Who leaves people like that?

Who sees the deepness and how heavy someone's heart is, tells them
their heart is the same.. Then disappears...

Who disappears?

Deeply Rooted: Seeds

Who plays this game?

Who plays games with people?

You came,

Made something,

Made me bleed,

We shared blood,

Got afraid, reasoned with yourself

Then left, like your father did,

Like daddy, like kid...

You shared ink with me...

We wrote our secrets and tears into that ink,

Then as my eye took one blink,

You were gone...

And I was wrong,

Covered in blood but still wrong,

Stuck singing this same old song,

But wanting the music to be turned off,

No, I wanted to burn that phone..

Where bloody pictures were stored,

I wanted to burn every last memory of you I owned,

Every friendship is flawed,

But it's heavy,

Having a frozen heart, and with every friendship attempting to thaw,

But somehow I always end up with the short end of the straw,

Blood pouring? Pumping?

My mind started pumping blood threw the straw, still frozen,

What blood? How much blood?

Where did it come from? Blood everywhere

My fear of bleeding out wasn't there...

It was in my head, I lost so much blood I never realized I was already dead...

Jamal L Jackson

ASHES

I've been hiding you,

I've been hiding something,

I've been hiding behind it,

I'm not even sure if I can expose it,

It's been years since I burned the memory from my mind,

It's been months since the last time,

It's been months since the last time I burned myself,

I never truly saw any value,

Value meant someone felt something, and I didn't feel anything,

I grew up, looking up,

With a chin down,

So far down, I couldn't hear myself think,

I didn't want to hear myself think,

There are times where I want to be left alone,

But I've never truly known, if it was only because I was left alone,

There were fire fights when I walked hallways,

I grew used to being burned,

But there were waterfalls under my eyes,

They never put out the fire, they only succeeded in drowning me,

So I plugged them.

I plugged my ears next,

With cotton balls,

Then with alcohol,

I rubbed lighter fluid on the temples of my head,

Deeply Rooted: Seeds

I wanted to burn this body, this temple,

So I,

I rubbed charcoal on my feet,

I sprayed aerosol on my arms and legs,

Then I sat there,

Waiting to combust,

To catch a blaze,

To die and let the fire light up my grave,

But it didn't,

I would try this 5 more times in my life,

Never truly sure why I couldn't catch a spark,

Alternative school into high school would be the first start,

I tried, still no spark,

I had friends,

I saw them torch their lives and I thought, "they are sure to torch mine."

To that I let a tear out,

With fear of drowning, I put the waterfall out,

College would be the second time I tried to turn a blaze,

I flipped through books in my dorm room escaping the failure, trying to escape the shame, I tried to escape the rumors that followed my name,

They were true, and that frightened me,

I let those misguided and classically trained kids, paint a picture of me,

I sat in my dorm room, flipping through pages so fast my fingers hurt, paper cuts and still no flame,

So fast, I could smell hints of ember, but still no blaze,

Without a blaze, I couldn't withstand the way they hissed my name,

They say the third time is the charm,

But even this time, a flame would do me no harm,

And I tried, I tried my hardest,

I couldn't accept the falling of my sister,

So I tried again,

This time, I saw the glimpse of a flame..

I was before a bridge, and briefly I saw a brilliant purple flame,

I tried to touch it,

I cried when I couldn't,

It was too far for me, but I felt the warmth of it,

It dried the tears, but it failed me,

I didn't want dry,

I wanted fire,

The third time, was up in flames, flames I couldn't share,

Without deserving it, after 3 times my life was still spared,

The fourth,

In my absence of mind,

Someone else sparked this flame,

I had become docile, and slow,

Believing that the flame wasn't the way I should go,

But he sparked it, and he sparked it well,

White fire,

Rarest of them all,

So hot, it built a chill,

White fire, was said to cleanse, to repel,

And to heal,

Heal demons, and spell out flaws,

Deeply Rooted: Seeds

I wasn't healed,

He just left me burnt, and laying there,

To crawl,

So I did,

That flame was split between two strangers,

One a boy, and one a man,

One molding, and one trying to destroy,

I, being the process, and my end result being the end result,

I believed molding was positive, and I cast away the destroyer,

I allowed the molder to live for 6 years,

Until it hit me, I was his toy.

Their flames burned,

But I didn't combust,

They left me scars,

Those scars grew to be the only part of life to trust,

Still here,

Scars, and still breathing,

Every person with a torch, after all my begging,

Still leaving,

Scars but still no burn marks,

Cinco,

El Quinto demonio del fuego,

Here,

The fire was here,

I hid from it,

I ran when I could,

I sat atop rubber shoes, to avoid,

The spark from light,

Finally the fire didn't feel right,

I ran with water,

And I walked in teardrops,

I ran until exhausted,

I ran until I dropped,

It followed me,

It laid atop my shoulder,

At every chance,

At every chance the fire to my eyes couldn't become bolder,

I was haunted by fire,

By flames,

I went to sleep, and woke up,

My eyelids contained flames,

I went to sleep, and woke up,

My thoughts couldn't bare the flames,

I went to sleep, and struggled,

I didn't want to wake up and play more games,

I went to sleep, and then didn't,

The 5th Demon of Fire was calling my name,

I woke up,

To a ring of fire,

My memories, cast to the side,

My thoughts, provoked only worry for the ride,

My limbs were no longer mine,

Deeply Rooted: Seeds

Only my eyes didn't betray me,

This time,

It was only my eyes that I wished betrayed me,

Open, then close,

Open, then close,

Open, then close,

In those moments I wished my eyes lied,

This fire was cold,

He liked to play with his meals,

He liked to play with his meals before they got old,

22, ripe AND of age,

He licked and hissed at the thought of what I wrote of him on a page,

He was my muse, and my value only in the pen strokes I used,

He licked and hissed, at the times and memories I missed,

He enjoyed his meals, and I would be no different,

Too afraid to run,

I sat there, in fear,

He hissed, and my eyes grew wide,

Too afraid to run,

I sat there, in fear,

I wrote about being afraid, and he hissed in delight,

I wrote about being brave, and his eyes grew wide and tight,

Too afraid to think,

I didn't,

I wrote about being thoughtful, and those same wide eyes, grew small and squinted,

Too afraid to breathe,

Too afraid to leave.

I barely exhaled,

So I wrote about air, and breath,

To that my breathing excelled,

I was too everything,

I was extra, and excessive,

It wasn't until the fire didn't scare me,

That the demon found my writing impressive,

He grew fond of his play toy,

Of his thing,

Living under my bed, with fire, ashes, and brilliance,

Brilliant enough to burn everything,

I kept people away, out of fear, for them,

The fire enjoyed me, but at the demons whim,

I couldn't protect people, as much as I tried,

I was confused, and conflicted,

How could this demon be the first one to call me "gifted"

I tried all these years to burn myself down,

It was only in this fire, the fire brought alive the moments I found,

It was in this fire, I found myself,

It was in this fire,

That I contemplated my suicide,

But it was in this fire, the only true moments I felt alive,

Time,

At the base of my feet,

Deeply Rooted: Seeds

Time,

Something no person can keep,

In time,

That demon began to die,

I dreamt of this day,

I thought of rejoicing, but to my surprise,

I couldn't,

I sat over the demons bed,

Asking question, after question,

Only receiving answers to two,

"What is your name?" I asked the demon,

"All these years, Why did you do this to me?"

The demon replied, "I have no name, I've only been called what you gave me."

"I did only to you, what you made me."

"It was you, who made me."

In a flash of moments, those memories I burned came rushing in,

I was drowning in water,

I was drowning in regret,

I was closer to death, than anyone should get,

I built this fire over the years,

I built this demon over the years,

I built this fire,

I built this demon,

I built this demon of fire to stop these tears,

I built the fire, to burn back my tears,

I built the fire, to burn back my years,

He died,

Ashes written using magic,

He died,

When I allowed myself,

To drop,

A,

Tear,

Jamal L Jackson

HEARTLESS

Beep, beep, beep,

The sound of loud beeps eclipse the room,

Everyone fell silent, broken hearts froze the stares of them all,

But one,

His heart began to beat louder as the patient's heart began to cease,

He,

He,

He began to give commands, loud but subtle commands,

The room bounced to the sound of his voice over the beeps,

Those beeps,

Beep,

Beep,

Beep,

The beeps that killed, these beeps meant death,

In complete poise he orchestrated their moves, their walks, their stares,

He weaved tightly woven webs to capture the debris,

He used silk and Teflon to sow shut the wounds and keep the blood from getting free,

The nurses to his left having decades of experience fell short again,

They saw the patients slowly fading skin, they couldn't hold the fear in,

The new nurse's assistant, the fear in her was persistent, her eyes defeated by it,

Beep, beep, beep,

She fought to keep it at bay, but in the room following

Deeply Rooted: Seeds

5 more of those beeps,

Beep, beep, beep, beep, beep,

Her courage ran astray,

There was betrayal in the room,

The wiring malfunctioned,

The electricity gave in,

The machines made their own choices,

There he,

There he made a choice following his own voices,

The room was in a silent panic, chaos at every peak, meet,

He was unscathed, he glided around the room,

Grabbing tool after tool, he flew to the left,

He touched every part of that room,

Whispers broke out,

"It's over, he needs to stop."

"The patients dead, why doesn't he stop."

He proceeded,

There was something outside of the room that he needed,

He needed this patient alive,

So he continued to glide,

Triumph in his step,

Poise and balance,

Military grade strength of the highest budget,

There were but two things left to do,

Beep,

Beep,

Beep,

"Stop, he should stop."

Panic had overrun the room,

"Find the heart, and touch it."

His glide halted,

In an immediate withdrawal, he mustered all that he had, using glasses given to him by accident, and electrodes part of him by flaw,

Fire at his fingertips with the goal to thaw,

This frozen and death stricken heart,

He closed his eyes and sent 1,000 volts of electricity through his hands into the patient's heart,

Beep,

Beep,

Beep,

Beep,

Beep,

The patient's body laid there still,

The body didn't move, fighting against the man who glided around the room's will,

He gave another jolt, with no response,

He backed up, paced,

Walking, at the edge of frantic,

He walked forward and walked back,

He went silent,

Beep,

The room went cold,

5 more beeps, for a story untold,

He ordered the room empty,

"There were no options" he said,

He yelled louder,

Screaming, "THIS BOY IS DEAD,"

But his face read different,

The room's emptiness was deliberate,

4 hours, and 20 mins had gone by,

The nurses became angry,

Yelling orders to let them in the room, and that they would go and gather the boy's family,

But he had none,

Or at least before today he did not,

Because after the nurses broke into the room,

The man's heart, is what the boy got,

The boy was stabilized and the man laid there on the floor,

It took 3 hours to exchange a heart under these conditions,

The man managed this, and left a letter for the boy's future living conditions,

He would be given all of the man's homes,

his objects, and his money,

He would be expected of nothing, but to share what was given to him today,

To share with the world,

This story, and the heart he now owned,

The letter held,

These departing words " Be Free, take your second chance and demand much from life. & above all else, if you ever have the chance, BE ME."

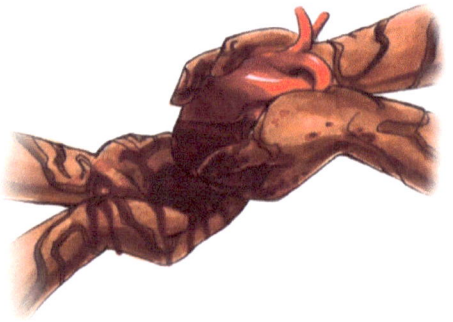

HEART FELT

Beep,

Beep,

Beep,

These were the only sounds I remembered,

I felt my body being pushed and pulled,

As if I was darting around the edges of a maze,

My life was but a maze,

There were lights flashing as I zoomed through these corridors,

I heard yells, and screams,

There was a group of people surrounding me when the zooming stopped,

I couldn't move, I couldn't see,

But I felt them,

I felt him,

I felt a strong presence, that of blinding light surrounded by a few other lights a bit dimmer than the first,

I could feel the bright light dashing around, clicking and clacking,

Sounds of metal tools filled the silent room,

It was silent but felt full,

Full of darkness, full of despair, full of disappointment,

Had I done something wrong?

The thought ran through my mind,

I knew I was here in front of these beings but I couldn't feel myself,

I couldn't feel,

I wasn't myself,

A shell,

There were whispers throughout the room,

The whispers came to me, so faint, distant, but close,

I made out a few words,

"He"

"Stop"

"Dead"

Was this them telling me I was dead?

Was I dead?!

Had my life ceased in these moments of dashing and whipping?

For the first time in my life, I feared lights,

Was the maze leading me to the cross roads?

I felt pokes at my skin, piercing me but with elegance and skill,

I felt a blanket of silk laid over my body for me to heal,

My eyes still wide open but unable to see anything,

I closed them,

Darkness with vibrations took over the room,

Beep,

Beep,

Beep,

Beep.

Beep,

The room fell silent again,

The heartbeats slowed down, all but one,

One beat faster, stronger,

That heart questioned my mindset and my mental,

Deeply Rooted: Seeds

Was this something I was actually going through?

I heard machines go haywire,

I felt wires being pulled out of me,

I was going cold,

My skin felt like it wasn't mine,

My heart sank,

My mind searched for it,

I felt an intense jolt,

Then nothing,

I felt another,

But again,

Nothing,

I felt the room go up into a roar,

Like lions dancing in the sun,

People dashing around, following the lead of that brilliant light,

This was brief,

The light kept going but the others fell short,

I felt relieved, followed by retort,

I heard whispers again,

Light, my last resort,

I heard the light order the room empty,

I heard, "THE BOYS DEAD."

But I was still there, panicking and pleading,

To hear me,

To see me,

There Alive,

The presences in the room dwindled down,

There was pacing and pacing,

That calm heart was racing,

That light was flickering,

It was caught between a decision,

Was it my life or the plug?

Was the light being called up above?

My body went numb,

Embarking on my journey upstairs,

Beep,

Beep,

Beep,

Beep,

Beep,

Hours had gone by,

I heard,

I heard again,

I could hear again,

The light was no longer there,

I felt warm,

Outside looking in,

The room was flooded by the prior presences,

The nurses began flooding in,

There was a flickering light again,

A letter eclipsed the boy,

He stood up,

Deeply Rooted: Seeds

Wires falling off him,

Blood on the floor,

Fully understanding what exactly took place,

The emotions, the fear, the gratitude, and the detriment.. all on his face,

This light was but a man,

A man no more,

Extinguished,

The nurse read the contents of the letter,

The boy let out a tear,

Almost falling to the floor,

He let out more,

Tears were all he could let out,

The heart that raced, did so for him..

"This heart of yours."

"You gave it to me."

In the ending of the letter,

This man gave his heart to you,

Only he was skilled enough for this, it took 3 hours to skillfully replace your broken heart,

He left you this letter, I've read most but please read this part

A nurse said as she pointed to the paper,

"Be Free. Take your second chance and demand much from life. & above all else, if you ever have the chance, BE ME."

The boys knees buckled,

Bent down, staring at the floor,

His knees buckled again, pulling him to the floor and his eyes to the sky,

The man whose body was no more,

Would now live on forever,

Through the boy who knelt on the floor,

Who was this little boy?

Jamal L Jackson

A HARD SPOT

I...

I...

I've been stuck here, I've been stuck here for so long..

I'm not sure if I've been wrong with glimpses of right, or right with splashes of wrong

I cling to the idea that one day, one day I will know if my feet are hitting the right marks,

The day I appreciate my scars... When I hold all the cards...

When the deck stopped switching, my shots stopped missing, my happiness, hostage or distant,

When loving myself wouldn't be so hard...

But I'm still stuck here, stuck between changing for the better, and what parts of me are better... Sick of this shit, hoping to get better...

I've written my feelings down, down to the last letter...

Writing until my fingers bleed, ink, or ink bleeds me,

Without feeling any better...

I can hear you whispering, hissing, faint traces of kissing... dismissing...

It's tempting, and I would,

But I've been swallowed by my thoughts, by myself, by this prison sentence,

And I've sat here, for years..

7 to be exact,

Every once in a while the doorbell rang, different people came in...

They still do,

Time spent, wasted timing...

Over time, my greetings started changing,

Deeply Rooted: Seeds

Hello, come right in.. (2-3 times)

Oh I've got a visitor, it's been a while, (4-6 times)

Hi, how long will you be here? (10 times)

Then the doorbell stopped ringing, and I felt knocks, damaging knocks, pushing the hinges off,

To which my eyes,

And hands began clinging...

Another Knock,

Door open... zero words,

To which I replied, "Duly Noted", I felt the door creaking as I began to close it finally,

But still here, open windows, no locks on the doors, and no security, just here,

I opened the door year after year.. tear after tear... developing fear after fear...

I opened the door, and never walked out of it,

Stuck waiting, debating on hating, myself, my self-medicating... my life lesson's lateness...

My death was patience,

I paid my mortgage faithfully, I'd dreamt of being homeless, of being home, less,

Of being reckless, dodging wrecks less...

Swimming in regret disguised as "the mature way to be"

Not hurting anyone, meanwhile being hurt myself...

I purchased the belt, whipped myself ten times, just so you would never know how it felt...

And...

Maybe, that's why being stuck here isn't my worst fear,

But that I'm stuck here without ever knowing what's out there, outside, my side, knowing my take, my why,

"Be brave. Be bold"

Words that have gotten oh so old,

Like my feelings, like this feeling, like feeling,

Words that have never shelter me from the cold

"Be brave. Be bold",

A story of mine, attempting to leave my tongue but can't break hold..

A story of mine, dead tears and blood fighting to be told...

But still stuck here

A loose door, open with trap doors, booby traps, wild animals, poison, and broken hinges,

A house full yet so empty,

Full but so empty,

Stuck here full but empty,

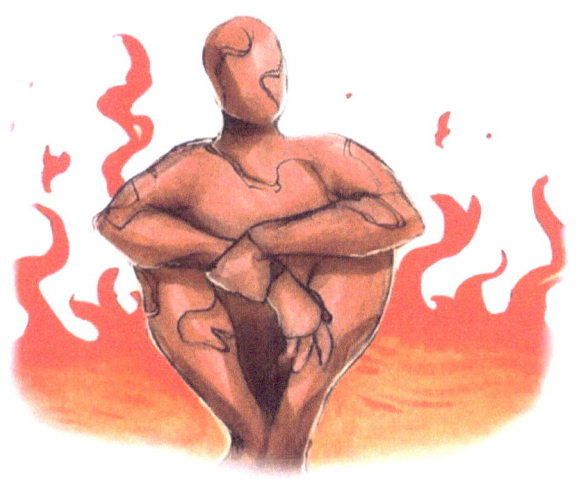

KEROSENE KILLER

"Some people need kerosene to burn friendships, I've done more with a match."

A call comes in, "It's done, send someone"

Dispatch, not sure what or who was "done," sent everyone they could. Cars pulled up, trucks pulled up, to nothing.

There was an address with no house, doors with no frames. Bodies with no names, a spot with no space,

There was a young man sitting there,

Early 20's at most. He was covered in rips and burns. Seeing the house and seeing him, he was covered in what he deserved.

His license matched the owner of the house but why, why burn down what your hard work earned?

A simple reply, spoken in a tone that wasn't to be missed, "A billion worth of earnings and not one ounce of importance. So it is now laid to rest."

Fragile and useless... are the objects of late..

Obstacles and bruises ... are what these objects made,

An officer yelled out, "but there were people in there?"

The young man replied, "they were dead before the house caught flame... I haven't the slightest clue to what causes are to blame.."

"This is arson, this is criminal intent.."

"This is a mistake, and the death penalty is what you'll get.."

The officer looked into the man's eyes... and saw the fire that claimed the house... felt the heat of the flames burst...

Silence followed the meeting of their eyes,

He understood the man's emptiness and how the flame quenched his thirst...

His first, but it didn't feel that way,

There would be no fear, there would be no regret...

There were moments before he struck that match...

Moments etched into his mind, burned into his eyes... the pain he felt when lips let out lies... to that there would be no match...

The officer cuffed him,

On the ride to the station the officer felt tension and his skin crawled with chills and burns...

The man was causing him to feel the burns, feel the house before it burned,

The officer reached for his gun, feeling threatened and disabled...

He tapped the trigger but the bullet and barrel were not able...

Able to carry out his wish...

Wishes without granting...

Demands with zero powers commanding,

A wish was granted, just not the officer's,

There was a ripple in the air, a gust that swept the truck...

So much that it flipped... and flipped and flipped...

The truck laid pent there for 8 minutes, and in the 9th minute a car came baring sirens and assistance...

Running towards the vehicle

"Dispatch Dispatch..?????!!!"

There's been an accident...

The arriving officer looked under the car, preparing himself in seconds to see dead officers and a suspect or them alive... he was prepared for the worst...

Or so he thought...

When he looked under the car...

What he saw made him fall back off his feet...

Face in awe, expression stuck from what he saw...

Another officer ran up after reporting the incident... asking the first officer on the floor...

"What?! Where are they?! Are they dead?! Are they dead?! ARE THEY DEAD?!?!"

He looked for himself...

Not one person in sight...

Broken glass shattered everywhere...

Truck lights going off...

But not one body anywhere...

To be found...

Within 5 minutes the truck flipped, for 7 minutes, and they laid there for 9...

Gone in 8 minutes...

Every officer's breath taken in 1 moment...

30 bodies burned down in that house... in 30 seconds...

30 people came crashing to the floor...

30 years in that house...

2 hands.. and 1 decisive choice...

There was but a trail of flames....

29 foot steps... leading away from the truck...

Ending in one thought, "Just how far had he planned this, and what exactly was the plan? Accidents or planned incidents? Surprising minutes or decisive moments? The answers were in that last flame filled foot step... and it'll only be answered..."

Leaving the entire station ... searching for evidence...

All they found were a bottle with one drop of kerosene in it.. and a match...

A note stating "I set it up in flames for questions, now set it up in flames for the answers!"

TRY AGAIN, KING

"People are named after storms"

But sometimes storms are named after people,

The people that come through your life taking everything they can, with them...

Ripping up your roots, and your grass,

Cutting trees off at the bases,

Whipping and destroying on any given basis,

I can still feel the breeze that snapped my neck,

The breeze that shook my bones,

I can still feel the breeze that snapped my neck,

The trees that blew my back out,

The need of yours in feeling powerful, when you kick my back out,

The trail of tears that follow the path of this breeze,

The angry feelings and violence you used to force me on my knees,

Forcing, me into me, my need to bleed,

It's hurts,

It's hurts,

It' hurts...

It' hurts...

It hurts you,

The breeze that was set into motion,

Being set into motion,

High temperature creating low testament,

Every day a testament to your broken temperament,

Deeply Rooted: Seeds

Bodies followed you,

Dead bodies followed you,

Venturous bodies followed you,

A body full of violence followed you,

A bloody body of violence swallowed you,

A twister set in motion,

A whirlwind set in motion,

A heart broken,

A heart, broken, set you in motion,

Sweeping the world of joy,

Searching for yours,

Sweeping the floor, searching for more,

It hurts you,

It hurts you swallowing up people, never being met by something you couldn't swallow,

Intentions hollow,

It hurts me,

To the bodies it didn't hurt,

You swallowed them,

In the eye of the storm,

I looked,

Remembering some storms are named after people,

Stealing, ripping, and uplifting,

You've met someone you cannot swallow,

And I repeat, you've met,

The one sided talk became a conversation,

I've met someone I cannot swallow,

Were the words escaping the mouth of the man,

Setting me free, from the breeze,

I've been ripping and whipping through,

Bodies at my feet,

Still, in fact,

No one considered my needs,

They ran from me,

Or they died by me,

They ran from me,

Or they died at my feet,

Dead at my feet,

Never questioning how to stop me,

Or how it affected me,

But today, in the dust,

I met something I can't swallow,

With closed eyes, and frantic,

I met someone I couldn't swallow,

I met someone I couldn't swallow,

I met someone I couldn't swallow,

You've met someone you couldn't swallow,

But try, try again, and try again,

You've been trying so hard, I'll commend you if you would only try again,

Try again king, I said TRY AGAIN KING,

You'll only be a king if you try again,

I'm not worried about you killing me,

Deeply Rooted: Seeds

I said you met someone you cannot swallow,

So try again king,

Keep trying king,

Try again king,

Try again king,

I want you to try until you cannot try anymore king,

I don't want there to be any dead bodies left after me,

So try again king,

Please to end the dead bodies, end this with me,

Try again king,

"That was when I was a whirlwind, and I met the king I could not swallow. The king that freed me."

ENIGMA

Backwards and upwards,

Forwards and sideways,

Are exactly how my brain allows me to live, to breathe,

Everything I've wanted fighting against everything that's meant for me,

My mind was fading in moments where I could squeeze my fingers into my skull itself,

I fought years and years to be who I was, manipulating myself to be like everyone else,

A chameleon of sorts,

Changing colors to match, and at most times, blend better than the ones I was matching,

A little boy,

Who believed he was designed to be capable of being everyone else,

Never truly understanding that he was designing himself to be this way,

The mastermind,

The culprit,

The sun, controlling light in the night time,

While it was the moon, that protected him.

Taking in sun dwellers whenever he could, thinking they resembled him,

Showing small glimpses of understanding, he began protecting them,

Exceptionally skilled in sympathy, but a master creator in empathy,

To a point where he couldn't turn it off,

Taking in stories, movies, and moments,

He was able to perfectly feel what they felt, or should have felt in that moment,

So, moments became his, most being only a fly on the wall.

He was the wall, the trees, the grass,

He was the roots, the air, the breath of the person he was listening to,

Beginning as a shadow over a shoulder, he would soon become that shoulder,

While lending a shoulder, he became a shoulder,

He experienced what you did,

Burns that scorched your skin, made him want to scrap his off,

Moments where you couldn't breathe under water, made him feel like he was losing his, breathe,

His thoughts became engulfed by events that required thoughts, and thinking, thoughts being rearranged, thoughts misplaced, thoughts exchanged, and thoughts encompassing, these thoughts incapacitated him...

Breaks weren't moments he desired, he needed them,

Breaks helped him from breaking,

But even in breaks he encountered more to take in,

Denying his feelings for years, he broke through,

And soon after he learned exactly why he had tried to abandon them,

There wasn't a place he could be without taking in what was around him, his mind controlled him, and his life,

It took in without discrimination,

Smell heightened, he could smell raindrops drip from leaves,

Sight enhanced, he could see the bottom of the ocean if he tried to,

Hearing elevated, he felt the pain from a pebble hitting the floor,

Mental awareness peaked, he could feel the eruptions and explosions in the stars, shooting stars shot him,

He felt for them, because he could feel them,

There couldn't be a difference in reality or make believe with him, because he could feel all that was within him,

Deeply Rooted: Seeds

And around him, but couldn't separate the two,

And not one soul,

There would be not one soul who could truly understand this,

To understand was to feel, to feel what he felt, and they could not,

He would attempt,

But this isn't something that one grasps simply by attempting,

Born with this, with him,

A superhero who couldn't feel very super,

His own life shriveled up from the intense focus on that of others,

Intensity in itself would mean nothing compared to him,

Disorders couldn't account for this, nor was there disorder,

This was order,

An order that could not be renounced or recanted,

An order that once placed, could never be misplaced,

Living a life comfortable by shadows while desiring the light,

With abilities that suited him well in the light, in the sun,

With the ability of those abilities forcing him to the dark,

My sun being blocked out by the moon,

Or was it the moon that was blocked out by the sun?

Associating the sun with light, positivity, confidence and courage,

Associating the moon with darkness, negativity, fear, and fright,

I associated all of this with the sun, while it was the moon that kept me safe,

The sun dwellers, were the bandits of the night. Killing, stealing, and diluting the presence of the moon,

And a question was posed, deep into the boy's mind,

Should the moon change it's ways based on the bandits ability and desire to take advantage of them?

If so, would the moon really have won?

Or has the sun actually taken over by influencing the moon's win?

Sadness wrapped into the shadows and happiness expected from the light of day,

Mental attempts to make sense of the madness in the sun,

To accept what cannot be accepted,

To accept death while living,

Or living while dead,

Moments denied from me,

I wanted my own moments back,

It was all in my head, and I just wanted my moments back,

My time back,

What was stolen, I wanted it back,

Every day was another moment trying to fight for my time back, I wanted my time..

Fights that held out until about 10:30 a.m.,

Battles that could be fought every day, and that SHOULD be fought every single day,

Small compact portals held in the hand,

Portals that took my moments away, in exchange for the moments of others,

Inorganic selection, skillful deception,

I wanted my moments back, sleep was a friend yet still an enemy,

With the ability to make me see me, while still looking at someone deeply,

I wanted to be alone without the loneliness,

To be quiet with the silence,

I wanted words without the edge, without the blade,

Deeply Rooted: Seeds

I wanted nourishment without the food,

Sleep without the dreams, sleep with no nightmares,

Internal sleep, not eternal sleep,

I wanted me, my back, I wanted the *Me,* that I was and once wanted to be back,

To be the little boy again,

But that little boy had no business in this adult world,

I tried to bring him back,

While he cried to stay far far away,

He walked many steps and paths, and he performed well, until the moments of others began to send planes with huge devastating bombs our way,

He ran to evacuate the others, going from door to door in the village where people like him lived,

And he opened each door, learning that everyone was already gone, vanished, into thin air,

He felt people but they weren't located in this village with him,

Having wasted so much time, he ran as fast as he could to dodge the bombs and the debris that tossed itself into the air,

His legs were tired and his arms were heavy, but not as heavy as his mind, which died a little with every footstep, with every jump,

Finally having found shelter,

The little boy curled up into a ball,

Screaming at the height of his voice,

Until even his silence was drowned out by the explosions,

Hiding in the basement meant nothing to sound,

The sounds of destruction,

The sounds of death,

Sounds that made his ears bleed,

The sounds that became best friends to his ears, only to stab him closer in the heart later,

His whispers became faint, and his abilities couldn't cure this pain,

The ball he curled into and silence were all that made him feel safe, or alive,

This sound and experience would last for years, even decades,

And him, still living in the basement,

Sound after sound,

Until it stopped one day,

Running upstairs, outside to freedom,

Or so he thought,

Living in a village where it's only inhabitants were like him,

In a village where, only he dwelled,

He grew uninformed, never realizing,

That he was this only villager because no one else was like him, and there would be no other villagers,

A fact that he has yet to know and understand,

A fact that he has yet to accept,

But accepting doesn't change it,

Times where people attempted to explain his situations to him, but they could not, he was an enigma,

One even he didn't understand, there would be no one to understand him, besides him..

He was alone...

Jamal L Jackson

GASPING

The air flew out of my body,

I tried to grab at it, but it slipped through my hands,

Something took the air I needed to survive away from me,

I felt this feeling before,

The feeling of desperation, of loss, of losing,

I was losing my life,

Just like everything else up until this point,

I felt the air leave my body like my chances at love, at leadership,

My chances at happiness,

No second chances, my chances, slight advances, desired enhancing,

I lost all my chances,

My body began coughing up blood, I choked on blood,

My lungs collapsed, but I kept going on,

My kidneys ran dry,

My liver gave out,

My eyes bled,

Body grew numb,

Blood back to blue,

& I fell to the ground,

I was hunched over,

Then a group of visitors came by,

My ears grew wide in relief,

I heard walking and I felt eyes on me,

But no warmth, no touch,

My body was cold, still cold,

Deeply Rooted: Seeds

Surrounded yet still cold,

Time went by and I lost my hope,

I laid there, still alive but slowly breaking,

And I felt wind rushing towards me fast,

I felt cold wind, a gust of it,

And what followed began to dig my grave,

A kick sharper than a hot steel knife through butter,

My insides felt mushed and weak like butter,

My blood spit up blood,

Blue to red, and red to black,

They blew out my back,

These kicks, sharp kicks,

I spit up my organs on that ground,

Cold desolate ground,

I offered whatever came out of me to steal,

Maybe they were here to take something? To get something?

I kept reaching and pulling out more and more and more and more,

And it didn't stop,

The kicking got worse, my pain felt worse, my sores turned burns,

My skin began to crawl, to pull off,

This time my heart was on the ground beating and flopping up and down bouncing around,

Cords connecting my blood and back to it, began to rip off,

It was all I had left, and I felt it snap,

.....

....

....

Nothing,

I felt nothing,

Numb again,

Numb for the last time,

This was my last time,

Numb,
from my past time,

The kicking continued, followed by boards and bricks,

The air that left me returned and I never felt it,

The blood was blocking it, blocking me,

My blood was me, blocking me,

My body being dragged,

I had nothing left to give, but they still wanted to take,

My life wasn't there anymore,

A fragile container of bones and blood, bullshit,

With smells like bull's shit,

This,

Crafted fit, bullshit,

It, this is it,

I saw my path off a cliff,

Descending slowly,

Winded, my flight time ended,

"Good Riddance"

I clung onto air, and life, never realizing my life went with the air the first
time it left,

ABOUT THE AUTHOR

I honestly cannot provide much here. I wish I could, and I can't. Who I am is written in the stories you just read and the ones you have yet to. I do not know who I am, my favorite color, food, hobby, or what brings me genuine joy, besides people.

From as early as I can remember, *people* have been all that I was good at, aspired for, of, and my connection to them. I do not know Jamal outside of what is deeply rooted within another. I want "to be alone, without the loneliness." Every line in every story has a meaning, a real meaning. None were picked for wow factor or readers. I was talking to myself in the pieces, it was my safe way of recalling what I tried to forget.

& I am sorry if this is a drop off for you, or I fall short in some way of what an "author" is supposed to do. I simply do not want to give you false truths or glamour, when I have none.

I am only Peter Pan when I sleep, there is no magic here. Dirt doesn't always hide diamonds, sometimes it is just dirty.

Thank you dearly for reading! If you want to share your thoughts or ask questions regarding the lines, their meanings, or their creation. Please email me: Deeplyrootedtheseries@gmail.com

For any additional merchandise or information regarding upcoming events/plans for Deeply Rooted: Seeds please visit www.neverywayjay.com

Sincerely,

Jamal Leon Jackson

I am no one while everyone at once. Somewhere while nowhere at the same time. I am me, you, and us. But I am not them. Never be them.

www.ingramcontent.com/pod-product-compliance
Lightning Source LLC
Chambersburg PA
CBHW041411010726

47507CB00001B/73